D0116626

Dear Mother, Dear Daughter

POEMS FOR YOUNG PEOPLE

BY JANE YOLEN
AND
HEIDI E. Y. STEMPLE

ILLUSTRATIONS BY GIL ASHBY

WORDSONG
BOYDS MILLS PRESS

To Will and Isabelle Yolen and David Stemple,
who made me a daughter and a mother
—J. Y.

For my husband, Brandon Piatt, and my daddy,
David Stemple, who are neither mother nor daughter
but made me both
—H. E. Y. S.

Text copyright © 2001 by Jane Yolen and Heidi E. Y. Stemple
Illustrations copyright © 2001 by Boyds Mills Press

Published by Wordsong
Boyds Mills Press, Inc.
A Highlights Company
815 Church Street
Honesdale, Pennsylvania 18431
Printed in China

U.S. Cataloging-in-Publication Data
   (Library of Congress Standards)

Yolen, Jane
    Dear Mother, Dear Daughter: Poems for Young People ; By Jane Yolen
and Heidi E. Y. Stemple ; Illustrations by Gil Ashby.—1st ed.
[40]p. : col. ill. ; cm.
Summary: mother and daughter converse through poetry.
ISBN 1-56397-886-5
1. Mothers—Poetry. 2. Mothers and daughters—Poetry.
3. American poetry—Collections. I. Stemple, Heidi E. Y. II. Ashby,
Gil, ill. III. Title.
811/.54 21 2001   CIP   AC
00-103867

First edition, 2001
The text of this book is set in 14-point Galliard.
Visit our Web site at www.boydsmillspress.com

10 9 8 7 6 5 4 3

Contents

Introduction

My daughter and I have always sent each other notes—sometimes quick little memos left on a pillow or inside a journal, or letters and postcards sent through the mail. Now that there is e-mail, we send each other long instant messages several times a day.

   Good communication is an important part of our family life. And we—the only girls in our family (father and two boys outnumber us)—talk, talk, talk all the time.

—*Jane Yolen*

I am the voice of the daughters in this book and the real-life daughter of Jane Yolen. However, I am not nine, ten, or twelve years old like the girls of the poems. I am in my thirties now, with two daughters of my own. So as they grow up, I hear some of the same questions and complaints that are addressed in this book (my younger daughter, Maddison, wants a later bedtime, and my older daughter, Lexi, won the phone-in-her-room battle). It was more fun for me to be the daughter again for a little while instead of the mom.

—*Heidi E. Y. Stemple*

Writing a poem about a problem that you're having allows you to break down the emotion into small enough parts so you can deal with it. Communicating with a parent in this way sometimes can be more helpful than talking.

   None of these poems is about an actual event. But each one is about a problem we have wrestled with as daughters, as mothers. And maybe—just maybe—you will recognize yourself, too.

—*J. Y. and H. E. Y. S.*

Homework

You just don't see—
Reminding me
Won't get my homework done.

Let me watch one show,
Then to work I'll go.
Won't you let me have some fun?

The book's been read.
The report's in my head.
All I have to do is write.

So I just don't see
Why you keep bugging me.
No, I won't be up all night!

Homework Police

I just don't see
Why I have to be
The homework cop each night.

If you planned ahead,
Had things written, had things read . . .
We wouldn't be having this fight.

But instead you wait
Till it's much too late
And our tempers are raw and rough.

Still—if I can't cease
Being homework police,
By golly, I am going to get tough!

Tuck her up,
Lock her up,
Cancel all calls.
TV off.
Movies off.
No more malls.

HOMEWORK POLICE—
HAVE SIREN WILL BLOW!

Fat

I'm fat,
I'm fat,
I'm helplessly fat.

I see the girls on TV,
and I'll never look like that!

I'm flat,
I'm flat,
I'm hopelessly flat.

You bought me a bra,
and I'll never fit in that!

Not Fat

In my sight,
Mother's sight,
You're not fat, you're just right.

And the girls on TV
Wear their clothes much too tight.

And you're bright,
Very bright.
You are bright and sized right.

Besides—size doesn't matter,
(No, you're *not* getting fatter!)
And you know that I'm right.

My Room

It's *my* bed—
Why should I make it each day?
It seems such a waste of time because
It gets unmade at night anyway.

They're *my* clothes—
So what if they're all on the floor?
I know which are clean and which are not.
Who says they should be in a drawer?

It's *my* room—
Who cares if I clean it or not?
It may be on the floor or under the bed,
But everything has its own spot.

Your Room

It's *your* bed—that's true.
But it's not a bed of hay.
I can't go in while you're at school
And throw the bedding away.

They're *your* clothes—that's true.
But bugs live on the floor.
So if you don't fancy ants in your pants,
I suggest the clothes go in the drawer.

It's *your* room—that's true.
But it's certainly not a pigsty.
Since it's part of the house
 where the whole family lives,
We must see it each time we go by.

Crush

There is this boy named Jason,
who sits next to me in school.
I think he's really stupid,
but my friends think that he's cool.

The clothes he wears are goofy.
His pants don't even fit.
He keeps saying that he likes me,
and I really wish he'd quit.

When he teases me at lunchtime,
it always makes me blush.
When he tripped me on the playground,
all the girls cried, "It's a crush!"

So, I did something plain crazy.
I took a double dare.
I kissed him on the cheek in class—
he didn't even care!

Crush Indeed

They call that thing a *crush*
Because it squeezes on your heart.
It squeezes on your stomach, too—
The upsy-whoozy part.

It makes the boys get stupid,
And it makes girls lose their brains.
It's a special kind of ailment
That is labeled *growing pains*.

Only soon as you outgrow it,
You will miss it, this I swear!
So as painful as it is right now,
Enjoy it while it's there.

Not Here

She was always here—
birthdays and holidays.
Never missed one.
Never came late.
Grandmas are like that.
Always a gift.
Always a hug.
Always a laugh,
rat-a-tatting
like the woodpecker
on our old pine.
Always the loudest cheers
hullabalooing
at my soccer games.
Everyone is at our house
crying over now,
laughing about then.
It's the first time
the house has been full
and she's not here.

Here

You wonder
how such a full house
can feel so empty
with only one person
gone.
Her laugh is still
here,
pressed
like flowers
into the wallpaper.
Every shelf
in her room
is full of history.
The long graph
of our family's life
is proof,
if you need it,
that she is more
here
than not here.

Dear
Mother

Music

I thought I wanted to play guitar,
but my fingers didn't agree.

And when I tried the cello out,
it was too big for me.

The piano seemed a perfect choice,
but I guess that I was wrong.

And when I tried a trumpet today,
I blew nothing like a song.

I need an instrument just my size,
To tuck right under my chin.

I know what music's right for me—
I want to play violin.

Dear Daughter

Practice

Tuba or cello or small violin,
The problem is never the way you begin.
The problem is never the size or the sound
But if you will practice the whole year around.

Guitar or piano or bass clarinet,
The problem is never what kind you can get.
The problem is not what you beg, buy, or loan,
But if you will practice each day on your own.

When I was a girl I, too, wanted to play,
But never liked practicing day after day.
I hope you are smarter. I bet you are, too.
So one violin will soon be here for you.

Play it for me, make it sing high and low,
So we can have music wherever we go.

Dear
Mother

Staying Up Late(r)

Can't I just stay up for one more hour?
I've brushed my teeth.
I've taken my shower.
Can't I put bed off for a half hour more?
All of my friends
and the kids next door
get to stay up till nine.
"You're a baby," they tease,
so I'm down on my knees . . .
           please.
              Please.
                  PLEASE!

How to Bargain

Just because all your friends stay up late in the night
Should I give you a break?
Should I say it's all right?
If they all want to jump off the top of a tower
Should you go along
For an extra half hour?

Please use common sense,
And get up off your knees.
I will give you till nine—
Just because you said *please*.

Too Old

I'm too old for a night-light,
so I've pulled the plug.
But the shadows outside
don't seem to notice
that I'm bigger now.
And maybe the closet door
isn't closed tight enough.
The hall seems dark
as the inside of a coffin.
Are those branches
scratching at my window?
I'm too old for a night-light.
But I don't think I'm too old
yet
to climb into bed with you.

Never Too Old

Did I ever tell you
about the wolves
that lived under my bed?
About the great dark bear
that lurked in my closet
when I was a child?
Even now, when I wake up
before it is light,
I remember them—
the yellow eyes,
the black growls,
the *scritch-scratch* on the bed bottom.
And I still long to climb in
with my own mother
who—even sleeping—
could always keep the monsters away.

21

Dear
Mother

What If It Happened Here?

We talk about what's wrong and right,
but on the news at night,
I see.

In the park where the dog and I walk,
the older kids love to talk,
I hear.

In the magazines the images printed,
nothing left subtle or hinted,
I read.

Yesterday in school, for fun,
in Jimmy's locker was his father's gun,
I know.

It could happen here.

Worry

I used to worry about the atom bomb,
or a giant meteor,
or the old lady next door
whose wild eye
never looked straight at you,
who we all thought was a witch.
I used to worry about footsteps
behind me,
tough boys with slicked-back hair
ahead of me,
and the children
starving in Armenia.
I could not do a thing about them.
But we will call the school
about Jimmy's gun.

Some things go beyond worry.

Nothing to Do

I lie on the floor
and stare at the ceiling,
trying to think up
something appealing
to do, but I can't
because everything here
is boring and dull.
It is all so "last year."
Not a game left unplayed—
the computer kind, too.
My life is the pits.
There is nothing to do.

To Do

There are books to be read,
There is homework to do,
There is violin practice
Still waiting for you.
There are miles, there are piles
Of clothes on the floor,
And the dog waiting patiently
There at the door.
There are old magazines
That you wanted to save
But will bury us soon
In a papery grave.
There is plenty of plenty,
Both old things and new.
Don't you *dare* try to tell me
There's nothing to do!

Dear Mother

Note from My Teacher

I want to explain—
I have to tell—
when class was over
and they rang the bell,

my entire class
was in the hall.
We started throwing
a soccer ball.

A window broke.
A teacher came.
When no one spoke
I took the blame.

I had to,
though it wasn't me.
I have a note
for you to see.

Note for Your Teacher

So here's a note
That says it all.
You did not lie.
I'm standing tall:

Dear Teacher,
I am proud this day
My daughter did not
Run away.

She stood her ground.
She took the blame
Though others, too,
Were in the game.

I'm not excusing
What was done—
Destruction
In the name of fun.

But that she stood
And said aloud
What others did not dare—
I'm proud.

27

Too Tall

My pants are too short,
and my shoes are too tight.
I've outgrown my shirts.
And nothing fits right!

Why can't I stop growing?
It's just so uncool.
I'm the tall . . . taller . . . tallest
kid in my school.

They call me a giant . . .
stilt legs . . . a bean pole.
It's not like it's something
that I can control.

If I could, I'd be shorter.
This whole thing just stinks.
Is there ever someone who stops growing—
And shrinks?

Shrink

Your father's a tall man.
Your uncle is not.
Their mother is nearly
A minuscule dot.

My parents were so-so,
My sisters, the same,
So no one in school
Ever called them a name.

And I am just average
As average can be.
Yet you will soon grow
So much taller than me.

Genes are peculiar,
And sometimes they stink.
But as you get old, you will finally
Shrink.

Phone Lines

Please leave me alone,
I'm still on the phone.
And, no, I won't hang up quite yet.
Do I ever bug you
before you are through?
Oh, yeah, and before I forget—
a call for you came,
didn't write down the name.
So let me please finish my call.
I just need my own
number and phone,
then I won't have to use yours at all.

Busy Signal

Every time that thing
goes *a-ring-a-ding-ding*
I know that it's really for you.
One day how I fear
it'll grow on your ear,
and then what will you do?
But to buy you a phone
and to leave you alone
with an implant of wire and plastic?
I can promise and say
that there's simply no way.
That solution is really too drastic.

Sports

Do I have to take gym?
Can't you just say I'm sick?
'Cause standing in line
when it comes time to pick
the teams, I am always
the last one who's chosen.
I stare at my shoes
just as if I were frozen
in place with two feet
that don't work as a pair.
Have I told you today
that life's really not fair?
So write me a note.
Call in an excuse.
I can't take much more
of this shame and abuse.
I've good grades in English
and math and in French.
When it comes to team sports,
I just sit on the bench.

No Excuses

I won't write a letter,
I won't make a call,
Gym's not just for kids
Who can hit a baseball.
It's great for your muscles,
It's fine for your heart,
And it's time that you learn
How to really take part
In activities meant
For a group, not just one.
So lighten up, sweetie,
And start to have fun.
(P.S.: I was always
the last chosen, too.
Sorry I passed those
bad genes on to you.)

Dear Mother

Inventory of My Pocket

1 blue yo-yo with a tangled string;
1 unidentified crumpled thing;
2 paper clips, one bent, one not;
1 gold hair clip I like a lot;
1 hard candy, slightly wet
(how it got there, I forget);
3 balls of lint from the washing machine;
2 half crayons—purple and green.
But not a penny, quarter, or dime.
Can we raise my allowance?
     Don't you think it's time?

Pocket Change

You think that money grows on trees?
That cash leaks out each time I sneeze?
That when your pocket has no change
It's time for me to rearrange
Allowance, which—I don't know how—
You seem to think means I'll *allow*
You money, money every time?
Give you some more?
                    Not one thin dime!

(Unless you do some extra chores.)

Dear
Mother

Can I Please?

I don't want to dye my hair bright blue
or get a nose ring
or a tribal tattoo.

I don't want to sky-dive from a plane
or touch a live wire
in the rain.

Nothing dangerous.
Nothing to cause tears.

All I want is to pierce my ears!

36

What Do You Think?

Some kids do dye their hair bright blue
or get a nose ring
or a tribal tattoo.

And you would be mad to dive from a plane
or to touch a live wire
in the pouring rain.

But if on piercings you want to start—
the first place you'd pierce
would be my heart.

Wait till your sixteenth birthday—and then
we will have this discussion
all over again.

Different

There's this boy in my class
who's different.
He doesn't fit in,
even though he tries.
Which makes him stick out
all the more.
I don't pick on him.
But some of the kids do
because he's different.
I want to tell them to stop.
But I don't.
Because I don't want
to be different, too.

Differences

There's a girl in your class
who's different.
She sticks out because
she has red hair
and plays the violin.
She reads a lot
and has a deep voice.
But no one pesters you.
Yet.
If you remain silent
around bullies,
the next time they may
pick on you.

About the Authors

Jane Yolen is Heidi E. Y. Stemple's real-life mother. She remembers a ten-year-old Heidi raising many of the issues that are touched upon by the girls in the book. Heidi has two daughters of her own—Maddison Jane and Alexia—and they sound like those girls, too.

Jane lives in Hatfield, Massachusetts, and St. Andrews, Scotland. Heidi lives in Myrtle Beach, South Carolina. To create the poems, they sent their work back and forth through e-mail, Heidi writing first, then Jane responding with her poems. Finally, they reviewed and edited each other's work.

Jane is the award-winning author of more than two hundred books, several of them with Heidi, including *Meet the Monsters* and *Mary Celeste: An Unsolved Mystery from History*. Heidi's short stories and poetry have appeared in a number of magazines and journals.